WHAT BOYS DO

To Mom & Dad—JL

To my family—RPJR

Books for Kids From the
American Psychological Association
maginationpress.org

Magination Press is a registered trademark of the American Psychological Association. Order books at maginationpress. org, or call 1-800-374-2721.
Design by Rachel Ross
Printed by Worzalla, Stevens Point, WI

Library of Congress Cataloging-in-Publication Data
Names: Lasser, Jon, 1970-author. | Paul, Robert, Jr., illustrator.
Title: What boys do/by Jon Lasser; illustrated by Robert Paul Jr..
Description: Washington, DC: Magination Press, [2021] | "American Psychological Association." | Summary: Illustrations and easy-to-read text affirm that boys can do all things—love, laugh, cry, feel, and grow—and that each is perfect just the way he is.
Identifiers: LCCN 2020042658 (print) | LCCN 2020042659 (ebook) | ISBN 9781433836794 (hardback) | ISBN 9781433836800 (ebook)
Subjects: CYAC: Boys—Fiction. | Sex role—Fiction.
Classification: LCC PZ7.1.L375 Wh 2021 (print) | LCC PZ7.1.L375 (ebook) | DDC [E]—dc23
LC record available at https://lccn.loc.gov/2020042658
LC ebook record available at https://lccn.loc.gov/2020042659
Manufactured in the United States of America
10 9 8 7 6 5 4 3 2 1

WHAT BOYS DO

BY JON LASSER, PHD   ILLUSTRATED BY ROBERT PAUL JR.

MAGINATION PRESS · WASHINGTON, DC · AMERICAN PSYCHOLOGICAL ASSOCIATION

THERE ARE MANY WAYS TO BE A BOY,
AND SO MANY MORE WAYS TO BE YOU!

SO TELL ME, DEAR BOY,
WHAT DO YOU DO?

DO YOU LIKE TO MAKE THINGS AND OPEN YOUR HEART?

BUILD ROCKETS, PICK FLOWERS, CREATE WORKS OF ART?

DO YOU SHARE A STORY OR SOMETHING TO EAT?
NOTICE YOUR FEELINGS WHEN
YOU GATHER AND MEET?

DO YOU NURTURE OTHERS BY HELPING THEM GROW?

DO YOU TRY TO LISTEN TO WHAT OTHERS MAY SAY?

DO YOU HAVE TALENTS OR
BIG DREAMS INSIDE?

HOPE TO DO THINGS THAT YOU
NEVER HAVE TRIED?

DO YOU PLAY ALL TOGETHER AND ASK FRIENDS TO JOIN IN?

WELCOME EACH OTHER WITH
A SMILE OR A GRIN?

DO YOU RUN THROUGH THE FOREST OR SWIM PAST THE SHORE?

FIND SAFE SPACES AROUND TO
WANDER AND EXPLORE?

DO YOU NOTICE WHATEVER YOUR
FRIENDS MIGHT BE FEELING?

SHOW THEM YOU CARE AND
THAT THEY STILL BELONG?

DO YOU SHOW YOUR AFFECTION AND HOW MUCH YOU CARE?

GIVE BIG HUGS
WITH THE STRENGTH
OF A BEAR?

YOU HAVE CHOICES
AND YOU GET
TO BE YOU.

SO LET ME ASK AGAIN, DEAR BOY,
WHAT DO YOU DO?

READER'S NOTE

Raising and teaching children provides us with many joys and challenges. While we spend much of our energy focused on the present with kids, we also think about their future lives. Who will these little people become? What will they be like as adults? We may also wonder how our interactions with them today will shape their development for the future.

In the case of boys, we often think in terms of stereotypes about masculinity. In many Western cultures, boys are expected to be tough, stoic, self-confident, independent, aggressive, assertive, ambitious, and insensitive. This gender role may be communicated to boys at a very early age. In fact, in one research study, adults were given the opportunity to hold babies in a hospital soon after they were born and they treated the boys more roughly than the girls.

Many psychologists and educators are concerned that gender role stereotypes can be harmful to boys and men (and to the people who live and work with them). Sometimes the term toxic masculinity is used to describe the harms caused when boys and men exhibit extreme gendered behavior including aggression and violence. In fact, some men may experience gender role strain, or stress from the challenges they experience in relationships when they are fulfilling their gender

role stereotype. For example, a man who does not express his feelings, refuses to help with household chores ("women's work"), and manages disagreements with aggression will likely receive negative feedback from those with whom he lives.

Research on biological sex differences suggests that there are few brain differences between males and females, and that much of the behavioral differences that we see are learned or socialized. Stereotypes of masculinity can be found in advertising, movies, television, books, and magazines. Many of our boys' role models also demonstrate gendered masculinity, and boys may be encouraged by others to demonstrate stereotypically masculine behavior. They may also be discouraged from displaying stereotypically feminine behavior.

Boys and girls may function best when they can integrate qualities that are masculine and feminine. Children who are given opportunities to be caring, assertive, emotionally expressive, courageous, nurturing, and strong are likely to have the qualities that are important for work, relationships, and navigation through life's challenges. When restricted to the qualities associated with one gender, children may be limited in their potential. Adults can facilitate the healthy development of boys by supporting their personhood rather than the more narrowly defined boyhood.

WAYS WE CAN HELP BOYS

There are a number of ways that we can help boys grow and develop beyond the traditional gender role stereotypes of masculinity. Here are a few suggestions:

Read diverse books to boys. Some adults may think that boys have limited interests and consequently select books that reinforce gender stereotypes. Look for books that feature male and female characters with diverse interests. Boys may enjoy books that show girls as strong heroes, or stories in which boys have opportunities to be creative and loving.

Engage in imaginative play with boys. Many boys enjoy playing in ways that may be considered to be stereotypically feminine. For example, playing house or school involves interpersonal communication, role-play, and imagination, yet many boys enjoy these kinds of activities. Through play, you communicate that boys can take on nurturing roles.

Support boys' goals and interests. All too often we assume that a boy wants to play a sport or play with toy trucks. Many boys do have such interests, and it's good to support them. Even so, some boys have an interest in dance or theater. Provide boys with a variety of options and support them in pursuing that which aligns with their interests. After school programs, libraries, and community centers often have programs, and an unrestricted menu of options for boys to explore.

Help boys see that there are many ways to be a boy/man. Though gender role stereotypes are powerful, there are countless examples in our communities of boys and men who have both masculine and feminine qualities. When you observe them, point them out to boys. For example, that man is holding his baby very gently. He loves his baby very much. That boy looks like his very sad. He's crying and talking to his father about his feelings. By drawing our attention to these examples in our world, we're building a set of lived examples of diversity in gender.

Practice unconditional positive regard for boys. We have an opportunity to express love and acceptance with boys regardless of their gender expression. Though some may criticize boys who deviate from gender stereotypes, we can promote health development by accepting boys for being who they are. For example, it may be shaming to say, "Don't play with that doll. Dolls are for girls!" Instead, provide a supportive observation, such as, "You're being very gentle with that doll. I see you're holding her head up so that she can see."

Boys can experience a range of feelings and behaviors. We can help boys by showing them that there are many ways to be a boy, and support boys for being who they are.

JON LASSER is a school psychologist and professor at Texas State University in San Marcos. Jon is the co-author of *Grow Happy, Grow Grateful,* and *Grow Kind*. He lives in Martindale, Texas. Visit @JonSLasser on Twitter.

ROBERT PAUL JR. is an illustrator and character designer. Robert spends his time mentoring children and teens and helping children lead enriched lives through storytelling. He lives in Houston, Texas. Visit steadfast.tv and @RobertPaulJr on Twitter and Instagram.

MAGINATION PRESS is the children's book imprint of the American Psychological Association. APA works to advance psychology as a science and profession and as a means of promoting health and human welfare. Magination Press books reach young readers and their parents and caregivers to make navigating life's challenges a little easier. It's the combined power of psychology and literature that makes a Magination Press book special. Visit maginationpress.org and @MaginationPress on Facebook, Twitter, Instagram, and Pinterest.